My Happ

by Julia Giachetti • illustrated by Helen Poole

I could not wait for my mom to pick me up from school. I got my bag and everything as fast as I could.

"What's the hurry, Olivia?" Mr. Tom asked.

"I'm going to my grandparents' house after school," I said. "And Mom said they have a big surprise!"

4

"Here's your mom now," Mr. Tom said. "Be sure to tell us about the surprise tomorrow!"

When we got to my grandparents' house, Mom told me to open the front door carefully.

Before I could ask why, a puppy jumped up on me!

"Meet our new puppy, Lucky!"
said Grandpa.

"Watch out for dog kisses," said Nana.
"We should have named him Licky!"

We took Lucky outside and played with his squeaky toy. He ran silly circles around me.

Sometimes he tripped over his own big paws.

"We knew you would be so good with Lucky," said Nana. She gave me a hug.

"We hope you will come over and play with him whenever you want," said Grandpa.

"Of course I will!" I exclaimed. We watched Lucky run around with his toy.

Then Lucky got tired, and he curled up in my lap for a nap.

"Best day ever," I whispered. I couldn't wait to tell everyone at school about my happy day.